Meet the Kreeps

The Nanny Nightmare
~◆◆◆~

Meet the Kreeps

Meet the Kreeps

The Nanny Nightmare

~❦~

by Kiki Thorpe

Scholastic Inc.
New York • Toronto • London • Auckland • Sydney
Mexico City • New Delhi • Hong Kong • Buenos Aires

No part of this publication may be reproduced, stored in
a retrieval system, or transmitted in any form or by any
means, electronic, mechanical, photocopying, recording,
or otherwise, without written permission of the publisher.
For information regarding permission, write to
Scholastic Inc., Attention: Permissions Department,
557 Broadway, New York, NY 10012.

ISBN-13: 978-0-545-06560-3
ISBN-10: 0-545-06560-7

12 11 10 9 8 7 6 5 4 3 2 1   9 10 11 12 13 14/0

Printed in the U.S.A.
First printing, February 2009

For Greg

*With special thanks to Jen A. for her
insight and encouragement*

⚜ Chapter 1 ⚜

W hat was that?"

Polly Winkler gasped and sat up in bed. It was the middle of the night, and her room was very dark. A thin sliver of moonlight shone in between the curtains in her window.

Polly stared into the darkness, her eyes round. She was sure she had heard something. She held her breath and listened.

All was quiet. And then . . .

Scritch. Scritch. Scritch. Scritch.

Something was scratching at her door! *Like a dog trying to get in*, Polly thought.

She froze, hugging the bedcovers to her chest. This wasn't the first time Polly had heard strange sounds in the night. Ever since her dad had married Veronica Kreep and her family moved into the Kreeps' mansion, Polly had hardly slept a wink. The gloomy old house, so dark and silent by day, seemed to come alive at night. Mice skittered behind the walls. Bats fluttered against the windows. And there were other noises, too — strange creaks and groans that Polly couldn't explain.

But this sound was new.

Scritch. Scritch. Scritch.

Polly's heart thudded in her chest. Although she was frightened, she was curious, too. She wanted to know what was making that sound. But she had a feeling that once she'd found out she would wish she hadn't.

Polly's curiosity finally won out. She climbed out of bed and tiptoed over to the door of her room. Kneeling down, she put her eye to the keyhole and peered out.

Darkness.

She put her ear to the keyhole and listened.

Silence.

Polly took a deep breath. Slowly, carefully, she inched the door open.

Suddenly, the doorknob was wrenched from her hands. Two glowing red eyes appeared in the darkness. As a pair of huge claws reached toward her, Polly opened her mouth and screamed. . . .

The monster grabbed Polly's arms. It began to shake her.

"Polly, wake up!" it said.

"Huh?" Polly stopped screaming and opened her eyes. She was lying in her own bed. Her dad was standing over her, gently shaking her awake.

"Wake up, Polly. You're having a night-mare," he said.

Polly blinked and sat up. "Oh, Dad," she said. "It was terrible. I dreamed that you got remarried and we went to live in a spooky old mansion with this weird family. And there was a monster —"

"Shhh," her dad broke in soothingly. "Don't worry, Polly. It was just a bad dream."

Polly sighed with relief.

"I married Veronica, remember?" her dad went on. "And you live in a historic old home with a wonderful new family — the Kreeps!"

"The *Kreeps*?" Polly reached over and switched on her bedside lamp. The room sprang into view. There was her beanbag chair and her white wooden dresser and her old desk with the crayon marks on one leg. Her clothes and books and toys were scattered all around. It almost looked like the room she'd always had. But it wasn't. Polly's old room had peach carpet and white walls and yellow curtains in the windows. This room had dark heavy curtains, a creaky wooden floor, and cobwebs hanging from every corner.

She was in her room in the Kreeps' mansion. It hadn't been a dream after all.

"Dad, could you do me a favor?" she asked.

"Sure, sweetheart. What is it?"

"Could you go look out in the hall? Just to . . . er, see if anything's there?"

Polly's dad raised his eyebrows. But he went to the door and opened it. "The coast is clear," he reported.

Polly sank back into her pillows. At least *that* part had been a dream.

Her dad came back over and sat on her bed. "Everything okay now?"

Polly felt as if she could still hear the sound of those claws scratching against her door. "There was a monster, Dad. It was so horrible," she said with a shiver.

Her dad patted her leg beneath the covers. "There's no such thing as monsters, kiddo. You're old enough to know that. It was just a bad dr —"

A ferocious growl cut him off.

Polly's dad leaped up from the bed. "What on earth?" he cried, looking around. "Did you hear that? It sounded like it was right in this room!"

"Um . . . Dad?" Polly patted her belly. "I think that was just my stomach growling."

"Your stomach?" Her dad sat back down, looking a little sheepish. Then he frowned. "Well, I'm not surprised. You hardly touched a bite of your dinner. You shouldn't go to

6

bed hungry, Polly. No wonder you're having nightmares!"

Veronica's weird cooking is probably what gives me nightmares! Polly thought. Dinner that night had been a hideous roasted monkfish with the head still on. It had looked like something straight out of a horror movie. Polly hadn't been able to eat a bite.

Polly kept a secret stash of peanut butter crackers under her bed just for nights like this. She had been eating a lot of peanut butter crackers since they'd moved in with the Kreeps.

But she didn't know how to explain that to her dad. He thought Veronica's cooking was delicious. In fact, he thought *everything* about Veronica and her kids was wonderful. He didn't seem to notice how much Vincent Kreep looked like a vampire. It never bothered him that Damon Kreep

7

did weird science experiments in the basement. And he'd never once remarked upon the striking resemblance between little Esmerelda Kreep and the family cat.

In short, he never seemed to see how truly strange the Kreeps were.

To make things worse, the next day, her dad and Veronica were leaving on their honeymoon. Which meant Polly was soon going to be alone in the spooky house with her weirdo stepsiblings.

"I wish you weren't leaving tomorrow," Polly told him. "I don't want to stay here without you."

"You'll be fine, kiddo," he replied. "It's only one week. We'll have our cell phones, so you can call us anytime. And Miss Pearl will be here to help you, too."

That was another thing Polly was worried about — the babysitter. "Why can't

Grandma stay with us?" she asked. "Or our old babysitter, Jennifer?"

"Grandma's on her girls' weekend in Vegas," her dad replied. "And Jennifer is busy with college now. I'm sure you'll like Miss Pearl. She comes highly recommended."

Polly sighed. She wished she could stay with her best friend Mike while her dad was gone. But Mike was away on vacation with his parents. He wouldn't be back until the end of the summer.

There was no way around it. Polly was going to be stuck with the Kreeps.

"Why don't you get some sleep?" her dad said. "You'll feel better in the morning." He pulled up the blanket and tucked it under Polly's chin. "Do you know what the blanket said to the bed?"

"What?" asked Polly.

"Don't worry, I've got you covered." Her dad touched a finger to the tip of Polly's freckled nose, and she smiled.

"Night, sweetheart."

"Night, Dad."

As soon as her dad was gone, Polly reached under her bed and got out a packet of peanut butter crackers. As she munched her snack, Polly thought about her problem. Her whole life, her dad had always been there for her. Even if he didn't see how weird the Kreeps were, things almost seemed okay when he was around.

But what would it be like when he was gone?

Polly didn't know. But she had the feeling it was going to be a real nightmare.

❖ Chapter 2 ❖

L eft here," Polly mumbled to herself the
next morning. "Or was it right?"

She stood at the base of the long curving stairway, looking from side to side.
Although she'd been living in the Kreeps'
house for almost one week, Polly still had
trouble finding her way around. The mansion was much bigger than her old house,
and the rooms never seemed to stay in
the same place. It took Polly ages to get
anywhere.

Not that she was in any hurry to get to
breakfast. She wondered what kind of icky

surprise Veronica had cooked this morning. Polly had another pack of peanut butter crackers in her pocket, just in case.

"Left," Polly decided at last. She turned past a carved stone gargoyle and headed toward what she thought was the dining room.

She'd only gone a few steps, though, when the hairs on the back of her neck prickled, as if something was watching her. Polly spun around. But all she saw was the ugly gargoyle. Its stone tongue dangled from its mouth in a fearsome grimace.

Polly made a face back at it. She was about to turn away, when suddenly a dark shape came flying toward her down the stairs.

"Heads up!" it shouted.

Polly quickly stepped aside as her stepbrother Vincent came sliding down the long curving banister on the edge of his skateboard. He flew off the end, landed, and glided to a stop a few feet away from Polly.

"Where were you going?" Vincent asked Polly. His face was mostly hidden by the hood of the black sweatshirt he always wore. "The dining room is this way." And without another word, he zipped off in the opposite direction.

Polly followed slowly behind him. She wondered if she would ever get used to living with the Kreeps.

Like most of the rooms in the Kreeps' house, the dining room was dark and gloomy. A huge iron chandelier dangled over the table like an upside-down spider.

Polly's dad and her brother, Petey, were already eating breakfast along with Damon and Esme. At the head of the table, Veronica was serving up plates of black, greasy-looking meat.

"You're just in time," Veronica said to Polly cheerily. "Would you like some sausage?"

Polly peered at it suspiciously. "What kind of sausage?" she asked.

"Nothing special. Just blood sausage," Veronica said.

"Blood?" Polly yelped.

"Blood sausage is an old German specialty. Try some, Polly. I bet you'll like it," said her dad.

Polly shook her head. "I think I'll just have toast," she said.

"Excellent!" Vincent rubbed his hands together. "More for me. Blood sausage is my favorite." He sat down at the table and started to dig in.

Polly shivered as she watched him sink his pointy teeth into the meat. Vincent intimidated her. He was as pale as a stick of chalk. He dressed in black from head to toe, and he almost never smiled.

Just then, Polly's older sister Joy bounced into the dining room, her clean white sneakers squeaking on the wooden floor. "Good morning! How is everyone on this awesome day?" she exclaimed, flashing a bright smile.

"Great until you showed up," Vincent grumbled.

Joy scowled and tossed her ponytail. "Vincent, do you always have to be so negative?" she asked.

"Joy, do you always have to be so blond?" Vincent shot back.

Veronica sighed. "That's enough, you two," she said.

Vincent and Joy had been squabbling from the moment the families moved in together. The two teenagers were as different from each other as night and day.

"Airhead," Vincent hissed at Joy as she sat down at the table.

15

"Grumpypants," Joy snapped back.

"Grumpypants," Petey echoed. "Is that one word or two?" Eight-year-old Petey was obsessed with spelling. He was always trying to learn new words.

"One," Joy told him, glaring at Vincent. "And it's spelled V-i-n-c-e-n-t."

Polly's dad cleared his throat loudly. He turned to Veronica's younger son, who'd been quiet all through breakfast. "So, Damon, how's the new experiment going?"

Damon's head jerked up. "What experiment?"

"Why, the new experiment you were working on in the basement," said Polly's dad. "You were just talking about it the other day. It was something to do with mice, wasn't it?"

"Oh, *that* experiment." Damon's eyes darted left and right. "Heh-heh. That's going just fine."

Polly's dad leaned back in his chair and folded his hands over his stomach. "You know, before I became a dentist, I was a bit of a scientist myself. You know what the most important rule of chemistry is?"

Damon's brow furrowed. "You mean, *When in doubt, transfer a proton*?"

"Nope." Polly's dad grinned. *"Never lick the spoon!"*

Damon's smile stretched a little too tightly. "Oh, ha-ha-ha-ha-ha-ha. That's a good one, Wally."

Polly watched him, her eyes narrowed. Damon had never found her dad's jokes funny before. *He's hiding something,* she thought. *The question is, what?*

"So, Damon," she said casually as she buttered her toast. "Just what *are* you working on in the basement?"

"Nothing!" Damon blurted. "Why . . . uh, why do you ask?"

17

"Just curious," Polly said with a shrug.

Damon gave her a dark look. "Curiosity killed the cat."

"But satisfaction brought him back," Polly replied.

"Oh, how quaint!" said Veronica. "In *my* family we always used to say, a potion of blessed thistle, eyebright, and boiled mandrake root brought him back."

Before Polly could reply, a screech went up from Petey. "Get off me!" he cried, leaping up from his chair.

Everyone turned to see a saucer-sized tarantula crawling up his arm.

Little Esmerelda, the youngest Kreep, hurried over to scoop up her pet spider. "Don't shout at Bubbles," she scolded Petey. "It scares her."

"Well, she scared *me*," Petey shot back. "And I think you did it on p-u-r-p-o-s-e."

18

Veronica put down her napkin and stood up from the table. "Esme, darling, keep your spider to yourself," she said sternly. "Petey, you have a wonderful screaming voice, but please keep it down while we're trying to eat. Oh, children, I *do* hope you can all get along while the nanny is here."

Her words fell on deaf ears. Across the table, the Winklers and the Kreeps were glaring at each other like two teams gearing up for a showdown. Veronica exchanged a worried look with Polly's dad.

"I don't see why we have to have a nanny," Joy said. "I'm almost sixteen. I can look after things."

Vincent snorted. "All you can look after is your tan."

"We'd just feel better having an adult around," Veronica explained as Joy stuck her tongue out at Vincent. "And Miss Pearl came with wonderful references."

"My old buddy Sam recommended her," Polly's dad said. "They were in the Army together for years before she retired and got into babysitting. Sam said he'd trust her with his life. She sounds like a real gem. Get it? Pearl? Gem?"

Polly's dad looked around the table, grinning. But this time no one laughed.

A sound like a lion's roar echoed through the house. It was the Kreeps' doorbell. "That must be her now," said Veronica.

Everyone else stood up, too. They followed Veronica out of the room.

Polly trailed behind the others. She was still thinking about what Veronica had said. What if they couldn't all get along while the nanny was there?

The doorbell roared again. "Coming!"

Veronica called. Her long black skirt swished as she hurried to answer the door.

Creeeaak. The front door swung open, its rusty hinges squeaking. Polly stepped forward to get a look at the nanny.

A second later, she stepped back in surprise. She could hardly believe her eyes!

⊰ Chapter 3 ⊱

Standing on the doorstep was the largest person Polly had ever seen. Polly's eyes moved from a barrel-like chest, up to a square, stubble-covered jaw, and on to the greasy black baseball cap pulled down low on the nanny's forehead. Finally, her gaze came to rest on the burning cigar clamped between the nanny's teeth.

"Geez!" Joy whispered to Polly. "I didn't expect her to be quite so big."

"Or quite so hairy," Polly whispered back.

Veronica stepped forward and held out her hand. "Miss Pearl, I'm Veronica Winkler.

22

We're so glad you've made it. But I'm afraid I'm going to have to ask you to put your cigar out before you come inside. This is a nonsmoking house."

Esme tugged on her mother's skirt. "Except for that time Cousin Hilda's hair caught on fire," she reminded her.

"Or that time I was trying to invent an edible smoke bomb," Damon added.

"Or every time Dad cooks dinner," Petey put in.

"True," Veronica agreed. She turned back to the visitor. "I'll ask you to please refrain from smoking unless your hair is on fire, or you are conducting dangerous experiments, or you are burning something in the kitchen."

The person on the doorstep tipped his hat back. Polly now saw quite clearly that it was a man. He looked at Veronica like she was crazy.

"Delivery, ma'am," he muttered around the cigar. "I've got here —" He checked his clipboard. "— fifty pounds of Muenster cheese."

"Did you say *cheese*?" Veronica frowned. "We didn't order any cheese. I think you must have the wrong —"

"Oh, that's for me!" Damon scurried out from behind his mother and signed the man's clipboard. "Please bring it over to the side of the house. I'll take it in through the basement window," he told him.

Hmm, Polly thought. *What sort of experiment calls for fifty pounds of cheese?*

As the deliveryman wheeled away the dolly of cheese, everyone suddenly noticed another person who'd been standing behind him, a short, rather stout woman dressed in a long overcoat. Her gray hair was pulled back into a tight bun. She was looking up at the Kreeps' house with a slight frown.

"Is this the Kreep-Winkler residence?" the woman asked. She had a surprisingly loud voice for such a small person.

"Yes, it is," Polly's dad replied.

"Then I'm at the right place," the woman barked. "I'm Miss Pearl, the nanny."

"Oh, Miss Pearl!" Veronica said, opening the door wide. "Do come in. We've been expecting you."

Polly's dad hurried forward to take the nanny's suitcase, but she brushed him aside. "I can get it myself," she said curtly. "A good sergeant always carries her own pack."

As Miss Pearl stepped through the doorway, six pairs of eyes watched her closely. The nanny had a pale face and small round glasses. Beneath her coat, she wore a flowered dress. Her feet were clad in sturdy lace-up boots.

The nanny set her suitcase down and looked at the six kids who were gawking at her. "These must be the children," she said.

"Oh, yes. This is Vincent and Joy," Veronica said, gesturing toward them.

"Teenagers," the nanny observed. "Lovely."

"And Polly, Petey, and Damon," Veronica went on. "And over here is . . . oh! Now where did Esme go?" she asked, looking around.

Hissss!

A noise at Polly's feet made her jump. She looked down and saw a little black cat with big green eyes. Its back was arched. It was hissing at Miss Pearl.

Polly had seen this cat many times. The Kreeps called her Esme's cat, although Polly had never seen the two together. The cat

26

seemed to appear whenever the little girl *dis*appeared.

Veronica reached down and scooped up the cat. "I don't know where Esme's gone off to. But you can meet her cat. You do like cats, don't you, Miss Pearl?"

Miss Pearl gave a brisk nod. "Good for keeping mice away," she said.

"Well, take special care of this one," said Veronica. "We consider her one of the family."

The cat hissed one more time. Veronica set it down and shooed it away. "Come back when you're ready to behave," she called after it.

"Golly," said Polly's dad, looking at his watch. "We've got to get going, or we'll miss our plane!"

As he hurried upstairs to get their luggage, Miss Pearl turned to Veronica. "Where are you going on your trip, if I may ask?"

"Bermuda!" Veronica clasped her hands together with delight. "Isn't it romantic? It's always been my dream to go sailing in the Bermuda Triangle."

"I see." A little wrinkle appeared between the nanny's eyebrows. "And have you left a list of instructions?"

"Here it is," said Veronica, handing her a folded piece of paper. "There's food in the freezer for supper, and all our numbers are by the phone. Please call if there are any emergencies — earthquakes, floods, plagues of insects, fire and brimstone raining from the sky, zombie invasions, werewolf outbreaks . . ."

Miss Pearl straightened up to her full height. "Mrs. Winkler, I was in the Army for forty years. There is no emergency I can't handle. Your children will be quite safe with me."

"Oh, I'm sure that's true!" Veronica said. "But I would hate to miss something like that."

Polly's dad came thumping down the stairs with their suitcases. "I don't know how you do it, dear," he said to Veronica, holding up a tiny alligator-skin valise. "A week's worth of clothing all in this little bag. It's like magic!"

Veronica's green eyes twinkled, but she didn't say anything.

The parents hugged and kissed their children, then hurried out the door. The kids watched from the doorway as they climbed into Veronica's long, black car and pulled out of the driveway.

When the car was out of sight, Miss Pearl shut the door. Then she turned to face the kids. She folded her arms across her chest. Her eyebrows drew into a fierce scowl.

"What are you maggots looking at?" she snapped.

The kids all looked at each other in surprise.

Uh-oh, Polly thought. *I think we're in trouble.*

⚜ Chapter 4 ⚜

Ten-hut!" the nanny bellowed.

The kids exchanged confused glances. "Ten-*what*?" asked Damon.

"It means *Attention!*" Miss Pearl barked. When no one moved, she added, "Line up, you ninnies!"

The kids shuffled into an uneven row. The nanny walked back and forth in front of them, sizing them up as if they were a bunch of new recruits.

She paused in front of Joy. "Neat presentation. Good posture. Perfectly imbecilic smile," the nanny declared.

"Thank you!" replied Joy, beaming.

"Joy!" Petey whispered from her other side. "Imbecilic means *stupid.*"

"Oh." The smiled dropped off Joy's face.

Vincent snickered, and the nanny's sharp eyes swiveled to him. Reaching out, she yanked off his hood. Vincent yelped in surprise.

"I've seen your type before," the nanny growled. Her face was so close their noses almost touched. "You have no respect. Which means *I* have no patience. Now stand up straight!" she ordered, thumping him between the shoulder blades. Vincent was so astonished, he did.

When the nanny came to Polly, she shook her head. "Freckles," she observed in a tone of disgust. "They hide the dirt. One thing I've learned is, you can never trust a freckled face."

As Polly shrank back, the nanny moved on to Damon. "What's your name, soldier?" she barked.

"Damon," he replied. "And I'm not a soldier, I'm a scientist."

"Well, Damon the Scientist, didn't your mother ever teach you to use a comb?" she growled, eyeing the prickly mess on his head.

"Actually, I used a comb just this morning," Damon said. "It's a simple technique involving static electricity —"

"Zip it!" Miss Pearl barked. "From now on, your hair should be so slick that I can still see the comb marks in it."

"But —" said Damon.

"No buts, soldier!" the nanny shouted. "That's a command. And you!" She whipped around to look at Esme. "What's that in your hands?"

Esme parted her fingers. She was still holding Bubbles.

The nanny's eyes narrowed into mean slits. "Thought you could scare me, did you?" she sneered. "I'll bet you were planning on putting that creepy-crawly down the back of my dress."

Esme shook her head. She cuddled Bubbles against her.

"It takes a lot more than a big, hairy spider to scare Sergeant Major Pearl," the nanny snarled. "I may be dressed in civilian clothes, but I'm no Patsy Pushover. I won't put up with pranks on my patrol."

Miss Pearl marched over to Esme, snatched the spider from her hands, and dropped it out the open window.

"But she's an indoor spider!" Esme squealed. She started to run after her pet. But Miss Pearl caught her by the collar.

"Trying to go AWOL, eh? Well, you won't get far." The nanny dragged Esme back to the line. She faced the kids, her fists punching her hips. "Now let's get a few things straight," she barked. "While your parents are away, I am your commanding officer. You do what I tell you to do. That means when I say, Jump! You say —"

"J-u-m-p!" Petey exclaimed.

The nanny's eyebrows shot up. "Think you're funny, do you?" she asked Petey.

Petey blinked behind his glasses. "No," he replied sincerely. "Actually, I've been told I don't have a very good sense of humor."

"Don't contradict me," said the nanny. "Drop and give me twenty."

"Twenty?" Petey looked worried. "Dollars or cents?"

"Not money, you nincompoop. Push-ups!" the nanny snapped. "Down on the ground, four-eyes. Hop to it!"

35

Petey got down on the ground. He managed two push-ups before his skinny arms gave out.

Miss Pearl rolled her eyes. "All right. On your feet, you pencil-necked geek. I can see I've got my work cut out for me."

Petey climbed back to his feet, looking embarrassed.

"Now, let's take a look at your mother's instructions." Miss Pearl settled her glasses higher on her nose. She unfolded the paper Veronica had given her.

As she read over the list, the corners of the nanny's mouth turned down. "What sort of hogwash is this?" she demanded. "'*Esme does not like baths,*'" she read aloud. "'*I would recommend against them. The children should not play outside before dark. If they go out in the sun, make sure they take their umbrellas. There's a lunar eclipse on Friday. Please wake everyone up to see it!'* Utter nonsense!" the nanny huffed. She crumpled up the list and threw it away.

"This is how it will be," the nanny told the kids. "Morning exercise starts at oh-six-hundred hours. Breakfast at oh-seven-hundred hours. I want you at the table on time with your faces *scrubbed*." She looked carefully at Polly. "Do not be late, or you will not eat."

The nanny began to pace again. "You will make your own beds," she commanded. "You will clean up after yourselves. During the day, we will run drills. It is my intention to whip you lily-livered lay-abouts into shape. At the end of this week, you will be tougher, stronger, and more disciplined. And you will thank me for it."

That is, if we make it through this week, Polly thought unhappily.

From the looks on the other kids' faces, she could tell they were all thinking the same thing.

⚒ Chapter 5 ⚒

O ur first task," Miss Pearl barked a short time later, "is turning you slugs into lean, mean machines. And from the looks of you, it is not going to be easy," she added, pinching Damon's plump arm. He yelped and gave her a murderous look.

The nanny and the kids were out in the backyard. The day was hot, and the air was absolutely still. Even the dry, dead lawn looked deader and drier than usual.

The three pale Kreep kids stood on the edge of the porch, blinking in the bright light. They reminded Polly of bats who'd been caught outside in the daytime.

"Now," said the nanny, "I have constructed a simple obstacle course." She pointed to a bunch of old tires that had been thrown down on the grass. Nearby, a rope tied to a tree branch dangled over a mud puddle. On the other side of the puddle was a small wooden sandbox.

"First, you will hop through the tires," the nanny instructed. "Then you will grab the rope, swing over the puddle, and land in the sandbox. By the end of this drill, you should be able to complete the course in under one minute flat."

"Miss Nanny?" Esme said.

"The first rule of training: Do not speak unless spoken to!" the nanny roared. Esme's huge eyes widened and she shut her mouth.

"I will demonstrate the exercise once and only once. I suggest you pay close attention."

"But Miss Pearl —" said Vincent.

"Zip it!" said the nanny. "Unless you all want to spend the afternoon scrubbing the latrines."

"Latrines?" Vincent looked confused.

"L-a-t-r-i-n-e-s," Petey whispered to him. "It means *toilets*."

"Oh." All the kids fell silent.

"Watch how it's done," Miss Pearl told them. She set the timer on her watch. "And — go!"

Miss Pearl took off running. She hopped through the tires, placing one foot inside each one. She was surprisingly nimble for such a stout person. When she got to the tree, she grabbed the rope and swung over the puddle with ease. She landed on her feet in the sandbox.

Miss Pearl checked her watch. "Forty-one seconds," she declared triumphantly.

"Not bad at all. Now let's see you sad sacks try it."

Miss Pearl went to step out of the sandbox. But her feet wouldn't move. Polly looked down and saw that the nanny's legs were slowly disappearing into the sand.

"She's sinking!" Polly cried.

Vincent rolled his eyes. "Of *course* she's sinking. It's a quicksand box."

"A *quicksand* box?" All three Winklers turned to look at him.

"I tried to tell her," said Vincent, shaking his head.

"What's it for?" Petey asked.

"Mother bought it for Esme to play in. But she hardly ever uses it," Damon explained.

Esme wrinkled her little nose. "Quicksand boxes are for babies."

The kids looked back at Miss Pearl, who

was now waist-deep in the quicksand. "Do you think we should help her?" Joy asked.

"She doesn't look like she needs our help," Polly remarked.

True enough, the nanny had managed to grab hold of the rope she'd swung in on. Hand over hand, she was slowly hauling herself up out of the sandbox.

"Wow. She looks s-t-r-o-n-g!" Petey remarked.

"And m-a-d," Polly added with a nervous gulp.

Indeed, the nanny looked furious. Her face was so red it was almost purple. As she stomped back over to them, sand spilled from the pockets of her dress. "Quicksand?" she roared. "Is that your idea of a joke?"

Damon's forehead rumpled. "Of course not. A joke would be if we'd put a giant biting sand worm in there."

Vincent chuckled. "That *would* be a good joke."

The nanny turned a shade of plum that Polly had never before seen on a human being. "I will not tolerate smart alecks!" she roared. "Drop and give me twenty. And I mean, all of you!"

Polly sighed as she got down on the ground to do her push-ups. She couldn't help thinking that things were going from bad to worse.

By the time they'd all made it through twenty push-ups, Polly's arms felt rubbery. She hoped that would be the end of their exercises. But Miss Pearl had other things in mind.

"This next drill," she said, "is all about teamwork."

"Ooh! I love teamwork!" Joy kicked one leg in the air and gave her best cheerleading shout. "Goooo team!"

Miss Pearl folded her arms. "This is not fun and games," she harrumphed. "It's about learning to work together in a real life-or-death situation."

"Life or *death*?" said Vincent, perking up a little.

The nanny nodded. "Now, this is a standard military exercise," she told them. "You must work as a team to figure out how to get the toxic material in Bucket A—" She pointed to a bucket sitting on the lawn. "— over to Bucket B—" She pointed to another bucket several yards away. "— without contaminating yourselves and without spilling a drop."

"That sounds like fun!" Damon scuttled over to Bucket A, rubbing his hands together. But as he peered inside the bucket, his face fell. "Hey! This is just regular water."

"Of course it's just regular water," the nanny snapped. "In a real crisis situation it would be full of toxic waste. But since this is merely an exercise — wait, where are you going?"

Damon was hurrying toward the house. "Be right back!" he called over his shoulder.

"Come back here!" the nanny bellowed. "I did not give you permission to leave!"

Damon ignored her and disappeared into the mansion.

Miss Pearl glared at the rest of the kids. "A team is responsible for all its members!" she shouted. "Since a member of your team has gone AWOL, you will all pay for his actions. Now drop and give me . . ."

The nanny's voice trailed off. She was looking at something over Polly's shoulder. Polly turned to see Damon dressed in a silver hazmat suit. He was carrying a metal container marked with a skull and crossbones.

"I've been holding on to this for a special occasion," he told them. "Who knew it would come so soon!" His voice was muffled by the gas mask he was wearing.

The nanny scowled. "What do you think this is? A costume party?" she snarled. "We are conducting a serious exercise!"

"Oh, he's serious all right," Vincent said, taking a few steps back. The other kids stepped back, too.

"Enough nonsense," Miss Pearl snapped. "Let's get on with it. Soldiers, as a team you must decide how to move the toxic waste safely to Bucket B."

Vincent, Joy, Polly, Petey, and Esme had a quick, huddled conference. Then Vincent stepped forward.

"Miss Pearl, as a team, we have decided that Damon should handle it," he said.

"Since he's got the outfit and everything," Joy added.

Damon nodded. He waddled over to Bucket B. Taking the lid off the container, he started to pour its glowing green contents into the bucket.

Only the green stuff didn't stay in the bucket. It melted right through it and burned a hole in the ground.

Damon peered down into the smoking hole. "Gee, I hope that didn't get into the water supply."

Miss Pearl looked from Damon to the bucket to the hole. Her mouth opened and closed like a fish's, but no words came out. Finally she blinked and gave her head a little shake. "Well, I think you've completed this exercise. Why don't we move on to our next drill," she said.

Joy smiled and kicked her leg into the air. "Goooo team!" she shouted.

For their third drill of the day, Miss Pearl gave the kids a navigational exercise. They were to be blindfolded and dropped off in a remote part of the wilderness. Then they had to find their way back with only the help of a compass.

Of course, there wasn't any remote wilderness in their suburban neighborhood. So the nanny had settled on sending them to remote parts of the mansion. In Polly's opinion, it would have been better to be lost in a jungle. *At least then I would have a chance of finding my way out,* she thought.

"I think there's something wrong with this compass," Polly said. She and Damon were standing in an unfamiliar hallway somewhere on the third floor. Or maybe it was the fourth floor. It was hard to tell. All the halls in the Kreeps' mansion looked the same to Polly — narrow, dark, and spooky.

Damon glanced over her shoulder at the compass. The needle was spinning in circles. "That's probably because of the giant magnet I'm carrying," he said. He pulled a horseshoe magnet the size of a dinner plate out of the pocket of his lab coat.

"Should I even ask why you're carrying that around?" Polly said.

Damon shrugged. "I always carry a magnet. You never know when you're going to need one."

Polly sighed and shoved the useless compass into her pocket. It was just her luck to be stuck on this drill with Damon, her least favorite Kreep. "So which way do we go?" she asked.

Damon looked up and down the gloomy hallway. "Beats me."

"But this is your house!" Polly exclaimed. "Don't you know your way around?"

"I'm a scientist, not a geographer," Damon snapped back.

Great, Polly thought, *we are going to be lost here forever. They'll probably find our bones a hundred years from now.*

"There might be a stairway around here somewhere," Damon said. At the end of the hallway were two doors. Damon walked over and opened the nearest one. Inside were stacks of neatly folded sheets and towels.

Polly tried the other door. A skeleton sprang out, its bones rattling.

Polly shrieked and leaped backward.

Behind her, Damon snickered. Suddenly, Polly realized that the skeleton was attached to a metal stand. Damon's magnet had pulled it toward them.

Polly watched as Damon stuffed the

skeleton back behind the door. Her heart was still pounding. "Why do you have a skeleton in your closet?" she asked.

"Doesn't everyone?" Damon replied.

Polly shuddered and slumped down against the wall. "I'm tired," she complained. "And hungry." She pulled a packet of peanut butter crackers from her pocket and ripped it open. Just then she heard it.

Scritch. Scritch. Scritch.

Polly gasped. "Did you hear that?" she exclaimed.

"Did I hear what?" asked Damon. He was looking around with a funny expression on his face.

Scritch. Scritch. Scritch.

"There it was again!"

"I didn't hear anything. You must be imagining it," Damon said stiffly. He grabbed Polly's arm and started to pull her down the hall. "Come on. Let's get going."

Polly shook off his hand. She was sure she wasn't imagining it. She crept down the hall and turned a corner. At the end of the hallway, something long and scaly slithered into the wall. Polly screamed.

Damon caught up with her. "What did you see?" he asked breathlessly.

Before Polly could answer, they heard heavy footsteps. A moment later, Miss Pearl appeared. "What's going on?" she asked. "I heard a scream."

"I saw something go in there." Polly pointed at the hole where the scaly thing had disappeared.

"Mice, I'll bet," she said, her lip curling in disgust.

Polly shook her head. "It was too big to be a mouse. It was long and slithery, like a snake. And it was pink!"

"A *pink* snake?" Miss Pearl squinted at the two kids. "An unlikely story. You're just trying to get out of the drills, aren't you?"

"No," Polly protested. "I really saw —"

"Zip it!" Miss Pearl ordered. "Drop and give me twenty!"

As they got down to do their push-ups, Damon glared at Polly. But Polly barely noticed. She was still thinking about what she had seen.

Miss Pearl is right, she thought. It couldn't have been a snake. Snakes weren't pink. And they didn't go *scritch, scritch, scritch.*

But Polly thought of something it could have been — a tail. A long, scaly tail. And she shuddered to think what was on the other end of it.

❖ Chapter 6 ❖

"Ten-*hut*!" Miss Pearl barked.

That evening, the kids stood stiffly behind their chairs at the dining room table. The nanny circled like a shark, inspecting them for dirt.

"Hands out where I can see them," she snapped.

When Miss Pearl got to her, Polly held her breath. She had scrubbed her face so hard she thought her freckles might actually come off. This was one dinner Polly didn't want to miss. After the long exhausting day, she was so ravenous.

A last the nanny gave a satisfied sniff. "At ease, soldiers," she said.

Polly sighed with relief and slipped into her seat. At the head of the table, Miss Pearl ladled goop from a big metal pot and passed the plates around.

A plate landed in front of Polly. She peered down at her dinner. It was brown and runny and full of lumps.

"It looks like d-o-g f-o-o-d," Petey whispered from Polly's right side.

"It looks like something worse than that," she whispered back.

On the other side of the table, the Kreeps sat with their hands in their laps. They were staring unhappily at the food, too.

"Is there a problem?" the nanny snapped.

"It's just that this isn't quite what we're used to," Vincent said. "Didn't our parents leave some food for us?"

"Oh, you want your mommy's food?" Miss Pearl sneered. "Well, too bad! I don't believe in coddling children. You'll eat what I serve you and you'll like it. This is good old-fashioned Army food. And you'd better fill up on it, because it's all you're getting until tomorrow."

Polly looked back down at her plate. Her stomach growled. *How bad could it be?* she thought. *After Veronica's cooking, anything should be good.* She picked up her fork and took a tiny bite.

"*Gaack!*" she gagged. This wasn't anything like Veronica's cooking. It was even worse!

Polly took a big gulp of water. Then she put down her glass and sighed. It looked like it was going to be another night of peanut butter crackers.

Miss Pearl was shoveling up the brown glop like it was ice cream. But suddenly, her fork fell to her plate with a clatter. "Intruder!" she bellowed, leaping up from her chair.

Intruder? The kids all looked around, but they didn't see anyone.

The nanny began to run around the room, locking the doors and shutting the windows. "Man the exits!" she shouted at the kids. "I want complete lockdown. Do not let the enemy escape!"

The kids were too surprised to move. *Has the nanny gone crazy?* Polly wondered.

Just then she spotted it: a tiny, frightened-looking mouse scurrying across the floor of the dining room.

The nanny grabbed a poker from the great stone fireplace. She began swinging it like a golf club. "Take that, you fiend!" she bellowed. The mouse zigged and zagged, dodging the blows.

"Well, don't just sit there!" Miss Pearl yelled at the kids. "Maim! Defeat! Kill!"

"But . . . it's just a little mouse," said Joy.

"Just a little mouse? *Just a little mouse?*" the nanny cried. She knocked into the table. A glass toppled over and crashed to the floor. She swung in the other direction and broke off the leg of a chair.

"Mice are vermin!" the nanny raged. "They carry disease. They have brought down civilizations. They are the enemy, and they must be stopped!"

The kids all watched her, dumbfounded. *Whoa!* thought Polly. *Either Miss Pearl* really *doesn't like mice, or she truly has gone nuts!*

Polly glanced across the table. Esme was sitting very still in her chair. Only her big green eyes moved as they followed the mouse. *If she had a tail,* Polly thought, *it would definitely be twitching.*

The nanny finally stopped swinging and looked around. She was puffing like a winded buffalo. "Where did it go?" she asked.

The mouse had disappeared.

Suddenly, Esme, who hadn't moved from her chair, gave a tiny giggle.

"You find this situation humorous, do you?" the nanny snapped.

Esme nodded. Then she brought up her hands from beneath the table. She was holding the mouse by the tail.

Miss Pearl blinked in surprise. "What? But . . . how . . . ?" she stuttered.

Esme got up from her chair. She went over to the window, opened it, and tossed the mouse out. "Bye-bye, mousie," she said.

Polly could have sworn she saw the nanny shiver. But a second later, Miss Pearl's usual scowl had returned. She righted her chair and sat back down at the table. "Finish your dinners," she told the kids gruffly. "Then go straight to bed. Lights out at nineteen-hundred hours."

"You mean seven o'clock? But the sun doesn't set until eight," Vincent protested. "How can we have lights out if it's still *light out*?"

"Open your mouth one more time, soldier, and you'll be on KP duty for the rest of the week," Miss Pearl barked, pointing a thick finger at him.

Vincent glanced at Petey for help.

"K-P," Petey whispered. "Kitchen Police. It means you have to wash all the dishes."

Vincent did not open his mouth again. Neither did anyone else.

When dinner was over, everyone washed up their own dishes and hurried upstairs. They were all in bed by 1900 hours.

Polly didn't think she'd be able to sleep with the sun still coming through the window. But before she knew it, her eyes had closed and she'd drifted off.

❈ Chapter 7 ❈

Polly startled awake. *Is it morning?* she wondered. No, her room was pitch-black. The only light came from the glowing digits on her alarm clock. *2:03.* Around her the house was silent as a tomb.

Polly lay there blinking in the darkness. She wondered what had awakened her.

Scritch. Scritch. Scritch. Scritch.

"It's that sound again!" She gasped and bolted upright. Something was scratching at her door — just like in her nightmare!

Wait a second, Polly thought. *Is this a nightmare, too?* She pinched her own arm, hard. "Ow!" Polly whispered. Nope, it was real!

She huddled beneath the covers, wondering what to do. The most sensible thing, she decided, was to just stay in bed and wait for whatever was out there to go away.

But Polly had never been very good at doing the most sensible thing. Once again, her curiosity got the better of her.

Polly crawled out of bed. She crouched down and felt around on the floor until her fingers closed around the handle of her flashlight. Then she tiptoed over to the door.

She hesitated with her hand on the door-knob. With a shiver, she remembered the glowing red eyes of the monster from her dream. And the long, scaly tail she'd seen that afternoon.

"It doesn't mean there's really a monster

out there," Polly reminded herself. "It could just be someone playing a trick."

Before she could lose the nerve, Polly yanked the door open and shone the flashlight out into the hall. "Gotcha!" she cried.

There was nothing there. The flashlight's beam fell on bare wooden floorboards.

Polly shone her flashlight up and down the hallway. Not so much as a spider skittered by. Was it possible she'd imagined the noise after all?

"But it sounded so real," Polly whispered to herself.

She was just about to go back into her room when she heard the floorboards creak. Polly froze, listening. A long moment passed. Then came another soft creak.

Someone — or some*thing* — was creeping down the hall. And it was trying very hard not to be heard.

Polly switched off her flashlight and tiptoed toward the sound. She was careful to avoid the squeakiest floorboards. Whatever was in the hallway, she wanted to find it before it found her.

When she came to the end of the hall, Polly paused. In one direction was the staircase that led down to the first floor. In the other direction was another long dark hallway.

The floorboards creaked again. The sound was coming from the hallway.

Polly's heart thudded so loudly she was afraid it might give her away. She inched toward the sound. The hall was so dark she could barely see the flashlight in her own hand.

Suddenly, she heard a noise, like claws scratching the wooden floor. Polly took a step back — and smacked right into something.

"*Aaaah!*" Polly screamed.

"*Aaaah!*" something screamed back.

Polly turned on her flashlight. "Damon!" she exclaimed.

"Nothing!" said Damon. Quickly, he hid his hands behind his back.

Polly's eyes narrowed suspiciously. "I didn't *ask* you anything." She tried to peer around him. "What's that behind your back?"

"None of your business," Damon snapped.

Polly sniffed. "Do I smell cheese?"

"Maybe," Damon said with a shrug. From behind his back, he produced a very large hunk of stinky Muenster. "I got hungry and went to get a snack. What are *you* doing up?"

"I thought I heard something," Polly told him.

"Where?" asked Damon. It was dark, but Polly thought she saw his eyes light up.

67

"Out in the hallway. But when I opened my door, nothing was there."

Damon peered past Polly into the darkness. "You shouldn't wander around at night. You never know what you might bump into," he said at last. "Well, I'm going back to bed." Taking his cheese, Damon headed down the long hall to his room.

Polly stood there for a moment, puzzled. Was it Damon she'd heard? But why would he have been scratching at her door? He hadn't seemed at all happy to see her. And what had he meant by *You never know what you might bump into*?

Polly turned to go back to her own room, when something glimmered in her flashlight beam. Two red eyes stared at her from the darkness.

Polly screamed and dropped her flashlight.

A claw clamped down on her shoulder. Polly spun around to find Miss Pearl standing over her. The nanny was dressed in a bathrobe and her hair was loose. She did not look very happy.

"What are you doing out of your bunk?" Miss Pearl snapped.

"Miss Pearl!" Polly gasped. "A monster! Run!"

The nanny did not loosen her grip. "What is this? Another prank?"

"No, it's right there!" Polly pointed. But the glowing red eyes were gone.

"You seem to have a very active imagination," the nanny said. Her cold eyes burrowed into Polly's. "I do not like imaginations."

Polly gulped.

"Now get back to bed," the nanny ordered. "Or you'll be doing push-ups til your arms fall off."

The nanny marched Polly back to her room. At every turn, Polly expected to run into a monster. But the halls were empty.

Once she was in her room, Polly turned on all the lights. She checked in the closet, under the bed, and in every corner. As soon as she was certain nothing was there, she closed the door tightly. She jammed a chair under the doorknob, for good measure.

Polly got into bed. But she knew she wouldn't be able to sleep. No matter what Miss Pearl said, Polly knew she hadn't imagined anything. There was a monster loose in the house. She was sure of it.

⫷ Chapter 8 ⫸

*B*am! Bam! Bam!

Polly opened her eyes. From the gray light coming through the cracks in the curtains, she could tell it was very early. Too early to get up. She snuggled back down under the covers.

Bam! Bam! Bam! Bam!

Something was pounding at her door. Polly sat straight up in bed, as the events of the night before came back to her.

The doorknob jiggled. Suddenly, the chair Polly had jammed under the knob went flying across the floor. The door burst open.

Polly was only a teeny bit relieved to see Miss Pearl standing in the doorway.

The nanny marched over to Polly's bed and yanked off the covers. "Up and at 'em!" she declared. "What do you think this is? Vacation?"

"Actually, it *is* summer vacation," Polly grumbled. She looked at her alarm clock. It was a quarter to six in the morning.

"Not on my patrol, it isn't!" the nanny barked. "Put on your swimsuit and meet out by the pool. Exercise starts at oh-six-hundred hours."

The nanny marched back out of the room. A second later, Polly heard a squeal and some grumbles from the next room over. Miss Pearl was waking up Joy.

Polly slowly dragged herself out of bed. She changed into a swimsuit and headed out the door.

Out in the hallway, she ran into a

bleary-eyed Joy. "Well, at least we'll get some fresh air and sunshine," Joy said with a halfhearted smile.

They heard a rumble of thunder. A second later, rain lashed against the windows.

Joy's face fell. "Oh, rats," she said.

When they got outside, Miss Pearl and the other kids were already standing by the pool. Miss Pearl had squeezed her stout body into a thick, rubbery-looking black swimsuit, and Petey was shivering in a pair of purple swim trunks. But the Kreeps were wearing their normal clothes.

"Where are your swimsuits?" the nanny barked. "That is not regulation pool wear!"

Vincent cleared his throat. "We don't actually use the pool, Miss Pearl. It's, uh, not good for swimming."

Everyone turned to look at the pool. Raindrops ruffled the surface, which was covered with a layer of green scum. A small frog was slowly stroking across the top.

With a snort, Miss Pearl turned back to the kids. "You aren't afraid of a little pond water, are you?"

"It's not the water that's the problem," Damon spoke up. "It's what's *in* the water."

What's in the water? Polly wondered.

"What's in the water?" Miss Pearl asked with a frown.

"We're not really sure," Vincent admitted. "But it seems to have a rather . . . large appetite."

Miss Pearl's chest swelled like a balloon. "I have never in my life encountered a bigger bunch of crybabies!" she bellowed. "Trying to get out of good, decent exercise with a bunch of tomfoolery and lies. I won't stand for it!"

Behind Miss Pearl's back, the frog had

started to stroke faster. Suddenly, there was a *Glurp!* The frog disappeared.

Miss Pearl hadn't noticed a thing. "Well, who's getting in first?" she demanded.

Everyone took a step backward, except for Polly. She was still staring at the pool. In the spot where the frog had just been, there were now only a few slimy bubbles.

"All right, Freckles. You're up," said the nanny. She grabbed Polly's arm and dragged her over to the side of the pool.

Polly's toes gripped the edge. She shivered, her knees knocking together. "Please, Miss Pearl," she pleaded. "I don't want to get in there. . . ."

"Hogwash!" thundered the nanny. "You're already wet. Stop whining and hop on in."

Just then, something dark slid across the surface of the water. It was gone in an instant. But this time the nanny saw it, too.

Miss Pearl's mouth fell open. Then she frowned and shook her head.

"It was just a shadow. A trick of the light, nothing more," she murmured. But her voice quavered.

Crrrrack!

A burst of thunder made everyone jump. Lightning jagged across the sky.

The nanny quickly stepped back from the pool. "Can't go swimming in an electrical storm," she said. She sounded relieved.

Then she seemed to remember the kids were still watching. She gave them an extra-ferocious scowl. "Why are you just standing there? There's nothing stopping you from doing push-ups in the rain," she growled. "Drop and give me twenty."

With a groan, the kids all got down on their hands and knees. Facedown in the muddy lawn, Polly couldn't help wondering what would be next. They'd been saved from whatever was in the pool. But the nanny nightmare wasn't over.

Not by a long shot.

⤜ Chapter 9 ⤛

Back inside, Miss Pearl went to her room to change into dry clothes. The kids had a huddled conference around the kitchen table.

"I can't take much more of this," Petey said. "My arms are killing me."

"On the bright side, we're developing good muscle tone," Joy pointed out.

"Forget muscle tone!" Polly exclaimed. "We've got bigger problems. There's a monster on the loose."

"What? You mean Mutt?" Vincent asked.

Polly blinked. "Who's Mutt?"

"That's what we call that thing in the pool," said Vincent. "I wouldn't worry too much — it hardly ever leaves the water."

"What *is* Mutt?" asked Petey.

Vincent shrugged. "We're not sure. It was there when we moved in. Mother didn't have the heart to send it away. She's always had a soft spot for strays."

Polly shuddered. *Some people adopt stray dogs,* she thought. *Leave it to Veronica to adopt a stray sea monster.* "I'm not talking about Mutt," she said. "I'm talking about the monster with glowing red eyes and the long, scaly tail, which scratches at my door at night."

Now all the kids were staring at her. "I've never seen *that* monster," Esme said.

"Well, don't look at me!" Damon blurted suddenly.

"No one *was* looking at you, Damon," Vincent said slowly. "But now we are."

Damon cleared his throat. "What I meant to say was, ah, without any scientific evidence, we can only conclude that the monster is a figment of Polly's imagination." He folded his arms as if the case was closed.

"Well, there's only one monster I know of in this house," Joy said. "And that's Miss Pearl. The question is, what are we going to do about it?"

"What do you mean *we*?" Damon grumbled. "It's your fault we're all in this mess. *Your* dad hired her. *Miss Pearl, she's a real gem,*" he sneered, mimicking Dr. Winkler.

"It's not *our* fault," Polly shot back. "We wouldn't have any problems with Miss Pearl if it weren't for your weird quicksand box. And your creepy pool."

"And Esme's tarantula," Petey added.

"I miss Bubbles!" Esme wailed.

"Hey! Hey!" said Joy, holding up her hands. "Come on, team. Let's pull it together."

"Joy's right," Vincent said, nodding.

That got everyone's attention. Joy and Vincent had never agreed on anything before. All the kids turned to look at him in surprise.

"We don't have time to argue," Vincent said. "We have to work together to get rid of her."

"Get rid of the nanny?" Petey asked. "How?"

Vincent sighed. "That's the part I haven't figured out yet."

"I could bite her," Esme suggested.

Polly shook her head. "She's so mean, she'd just bite you back."

"There's always smiling," Joy piped up. "You know, a cheerleader's smile is her first line of defense."

"Brilliant idea, Joy," Vincent said, rolling his eyes. "We'll just *smile* at her until she gives up and leaves."

Joy tossed her ponytail. "Well, it works in a spirit war," she said huffily.

"What's a spirit war?" asked Damon, suddenly looking interested.

Joy's blue eyes widened. "You don't know? Oh, my gosh! A spirit war is *the most fun ever*! It's when two teams cheer back and forth. And the team with the most spirit wins!" She looked ready to bounce out of her chair with excitement.

Damon curled his lip in disgust. "You mean there aren't any ghostly spirits?"

"No," said Joy. "But there's a lot of *team* spirit!"

"Spirits." Polly screwed up her eyes,

thinking. Damon had given her an idea. "Maybe that's just what we need," she said. "A spirit war — with real spirits."

"We don't have any." Vincent shook his head sadly. "Not even so much as a poltergeist. I wish we did. But Mother says haunted houses are really expensive these days."

Thank goodness for that! Polly thought with a shiver. "That's not exactly what I meant," she told Vincent. "I was thinking that we could *pretend* there are spirits and scare her away."

"Do you think that will work?" Joy asked doubtfully. "Miss Pearl doesn't seem like she's scared by much."

"I think maybe she's not as tough as she seems," said Polly, remembering the look on the nanny's face that morning. "Listen, I have an idea. Vincent, we'll need your skateboard. And Damon, do you still have any of those smoke bombs? Now, here's what we should do. . . ."

The kids all leaned in closer as Polly whispered her plan.

"It might work," Vincent said when she was done.

"So, are you in?" Polly asked.

All the kids nodded.

"But I still say it never hurts to smile," Joy added.

There was only one hitch to Polly's plan. If Miss Pearl made them drill outside all day again, they'd never have a chance to get things ready. But luckily, the rain continued to pour. Right after breakfast, Miss Pearl set them to cleaning the house.

"No wonder you're all a bunch of worms! You're living in dirt!" she bellowed. "I want these barracks spotless! We will have a spot check at seventeen-hundred hours. By then, this place had better be so clean you could eat off the floor."

For once, no one complained. Cleaning the house would give them the perfect opportunity to carry out Polly's plan.

A couple times Polly thought they were caught. Once, Miss Pearl came up behind her while she was rummaging around in a closet. "What's going on here?" the nanny barked, almost scaring Polly out of her skin.

"Just looking for another broom!" Polly said, hastily shoving the closet door closed. "Guess I got the wrong closet."

Miss Pearl frowned. But all she said was, "Well, get back to work."

Another time, Miss Pearl caught Vincent riding his skateboard down the hallway. "What on earth do you think you are doing?" she bellowed.

Vincent quickly kicked his skateboard into his hands. "I just found this piece of garbage," he said, holding up the skateboard. "I was taking it out to the trash as quickly as possible."

Miss Pearl gave an approving nod. "I've always said those things were for hooligans. Carry on, soldier."

By that afternoon, everything was in place. The thunderstorm had gotten worse, too. Lightning flashed, and claps of thunder rattled the windows. The mansion had never seemed spookier.

I couldn't have planned it better if I'd tried, Polly thought.

She crept to the closet at the top of the stairs on the second floor. Damon was already there.

"Have you got the magnet?" Polly asked as she crouched down next to him.

Damon held it up. "I always say, *Never leave the lab without it.*"

At the other end of the hall, Joy and Vincent were hiding in the closet with the skeleton Polly had found. That afternoon, they'd dressed the old bones up in one of Veronica's long, hooded black cloaks. Then they'd strapped the base of the skeleton's stand to Vincent's skateboard. The cloak hid the skateboard. When it rolled, it looked like the skeleton was gliding above the floor.

Petey was stationed in a bathroom halfway between the two closets. If anything went wrong, it was his job to throw a smoke bomb. This would create a smoke screen so the kids could escape before the nanny realized what had happened.

The Kreeps had decided that Esme should be the lookout. She was the only one who could slip past the nanny without being noticed.

A cat screeched, sending chills down Polly's spine. "That's the signal!" she whispered. "Miss Pearl must be coming now."

Sure enough, there were heavy footsteps on the stairs. She could hear Miss Pearl muttering, "Where did those brats go off to now?"

Polly opened the closet door just a hair. She could just see the top of the stairway. A second later, Miss Pearl came into view. "It's showtime!" Polly whispered.

Just as Miss Pearl reached the top of the stairs, the closet door slowly creaked open. The nanny glanced up in surprise as a tall figure in a long dark cloak emerged from the closet. Beneath its black hood, the yellowed skull grinned.

From where she was crouched, Polly couldn't see the nanny's face. But she heard her gasp. The nanny took a step backward.

"Now!" Polly whispered to Damon.

Damon raised the magnet. As he did, the skeleton's hands lifted. The skeleton began to glide across the floor, its arms outstretched. It was being pulled by two small magnets they'd glued to its hands. But the nanny didn't know that. To her, it looked like it was reaching right for her!

"Your time is up," Vincent moaned from the other closet in a spooky voice. He used Joy's cheerleading megaphone to project his voice. It sounded like it was coming right from the skeleton!

Miss Pearl gave a terrified cry and turned to run. Inside the closet, Polly grinned. The plan was working!

Just then, the skateboard hit a bump in the floor. The skeleton swerved sideways and bounced off the wall. It fell over with a clatter.

"Oh, no!" Polly groaned.

"Huh?" The nanny turned and looked behind her. The skeleton was lying on the ground. But it didn't stop moving. It continued to slide along the floor, arms outstretched, dragging the skateboard behind it.

"The magnet's too strong!" Polly hissed at Damon. "Abort mission!"

But it was too late. The skeleton zipped right past Miss Pearl, heading for the closet. Miss Pearl followed it with her eyes. She didn't look scared anymore.

"We're busted!" Polly groaned.

"Where is Petey with that smoke bomb?" Damon muttered.

They could hear Miss Pearl's heavy footsteps coming toward them. A second later, the closet door flew open. Miss Pearl glowered down at them.

"You!" she roared, her jowls shaking. "You . . . you . . . TWERPS are DEAD MEAT!"

There was a *thunk,* then a *whoosh.* Smoke filled the hallway.

Finally! Polly thought. As Miss Pearl turned to look behind her, Polly and Damon saw their chance. They squeezed past her into the hall.

"Oh, no. You're not getting away this time!" the nanny bellowed.

The smoke was so thick Polly couldn't see anything. All around, she could hear coughing and scuffling as the other kids scattered. Polly swerved through the haze. She didn't even know which way she was going. She could hear the nanny's boots clomping after her.

Suddenly, a large shape rose up in front of her. Polly skidded to a stop. Two huge red eyes were peering at her through the smoky mist.

❧ Chapter 10 ❦

I t's the monster!" Polly screamed.

Miss Pearl grabbed the back of Polly's shirt. "I've had enough of your nonsense. By the time I'm through with you, missy, you're going to wish you never heard the word . . . MONSTER!"

A creature had emerged from the smoke. It had a furry white face, red eyes, and two huge pink ears.

It looked like a mouse. But it was the size of a German shepherd!

"Monster!" Miss Pearl screamed again.

She let go of Polly's shirt and fled. Polly wanted to run, too, but she was frozen to the spot. The giant mouse crept closer to her. It wiggled its nose, sniffing.

I hope it doesn't think I'm a piece of cheese! Polly thought.

Just then, she remembered the peanut butter crackers in her pocket. She pulled them out. The mouse raised its head.

"Fetch!" Polly yelled. She threw the packet of crackers as hard as she could. As the mouse turned and scampered after them, Polly ran.

As Polly came charging down the stairs, she found all the other kids standing near the front door. They looked at her with expressions of amazement.

"Run!" Polly cried when she saw them. "There's a monster!"

"It's okay, Polly," Joy said, grabbing her arm. "You can drop the act now. Miss Pearl is gone."

"What?" Polly was so surprised that for

93

a second she forgot about the mouse. "What do you mean *gone*?"

"She ran out of the house scream-ing *Monster!* She didn't even stop to get her things," Petey reported. "It was a-w-e-s-o-m-e!"

"Whatever trick you played on her really worked," Vincent added.

"It was no trick!" Polly exclaimed. "We have to get out of here. There's a monster mouse on the loose!"

"Did you say *mouse*?" Joy started to laugh. "Who knew mean old Miss Pearl would be scared away by a mouse?"

"This wasn't just any mouse," Polly said. "It was enormous!"

"This I've got to see," said Vincent. He started back up the stairs. The rest of the kids followed him. Polly trailed reluctantly behind. She didn't want to see the big mouse again. But she didn't want to be alone in the house, either.

"So where is this mouse?" Vincent asked.

The kids looked around. Just then a tiny mouse darted across the hall.

"It's not even that big," Petey remarked.

"That's not the mouse," Polly told them. "The one I saw was at least as big as a dog!"

All the kids looked at her like she was crazy, except Damon, who had a funny look on his face. "Scientifically speaking, that's . . . er, preposterous," he declared. "Mice don't ever get that big. Er, naturally, that is."

Joy laughed again and shook her head. "Polly," she said, "you have such an imagination."

Later that afternoon, the kids were hanging out in the living room when they heard keys jingle in the lock. Everyone sat up and exchanged worried looks. Had Miss Pearl decided to come back?

The front door opened, and Polly's dad and Veronica walked in. Polly's dad was carrying their suitcases. Veronica was carrying Bubbles.

"Dad!" Polly, Petey, and Joy exclaimed in unison, leaping up.

"Mother!" Vincent and Damon cried, getting up, too.

"Bubbles!" squealed Esme.

"I found her hiding in a thorn bush out front," Veronica told Esme. "Darling, you know better than to let her get outside. Bubbles is an indoor spider."

"What are you doing home?" Joy asked as she hugged her dad. "You're not supposed to be back until Saturday."

"Change of plans," he replied. His face was pink and his nose was peeling from sunburn.

"Bermuda was dreadful," Veronica explained. "All that sunshine. It's so nice to be back in some decent weather," she added, shaking the raindrops off her long, black hair.

Polly's dad looked around. "Where's Miss Pearl?" he asked.

The kids all looked at each other. "There was a change of plans there, too," Joy said. "Miss Pearl had to leave."

"What? She just left you here? All by yourselves?" Polly's dad exclaimed.

"Don't worry, Dad. We were fine. I told you I could handle things," said Joy.

Vincent rolled his eyes. "Like *you* handled anything, Joy."

"What? And you were such a genius, Mr. Sourpuss?" she shot back.

"I see nothing has changed around here," Veronica said, as Joy and Vincent glared at each other. She sat down on the sofa and sighed. "I'm exhausted. Maybe we should just order in tonight. How does pizza sound to everyone?"

Polly grinned. "That is the best idea I've heard all week."

Later that night, Polly lay in bed. Her belly was full of pizza, and she felt warm and happy. She was just drifting off to sleep when she heard a sound.

Scritch. Scritch. Scritch.

"Not again!" Polly threw back the covers and climbed out of bed. She went to the door and looked out.

The hall was empty. *Maybe everyone else*

is right, Polly thought. *Maybe I really am imagining things.*

Just then, she caught a flash of movement out of the corner of her eye. She looked over and saw a long, pink tail disappearing around the corner.

A moment later, she heard the floorboards creak. Damon came sneaking down the hall. He was holding another big piece of cheese. "Here, mousie! Come to Damon," he whispered as he rounded the corner.

Am I imagining this, too? Polly thought. She went to pinch herself. Instead, Polly shut her door tight and went back to bed.

And for the first time since she'd moved in with the Kreeps, she fell sound asleep.

Polly's adventures with the
Kreeps continue in

Meet the Kreeps #4:
The Mad Scientist

Turn the page for a sneak
peek . . . if you dare!

L later that night, Polly sat in her room, trying to come up with her science project. It had to be something really good.

No, better than good, she thought. *It has to be great.*

Polly took out a pencil and notebook so she could write down her ideas. She sat for a long time looking at the blank paper.

Mr. Crane had told the class that if they were having trouble thinking of a project, they should start with a question. Something they'd always wondered about. "Being a scientist is a lot like being a detective," he'd said. "You follow the clues until you think you have an answer."

Polly wrote down the first question that popped into her head: *Why is Damon such a jerk?*

It was a good question. But try as she

might, Polly couldn't think of a scientific way to prove the answer.

Polly wrote down her next question: *What was that slimy, green stuff at dinner tonight?*

She tapped her pencil against the paper. She *could* think of how to get to the bottom of that one. But she wasn't sure she wanted to.

And besides, she needed something more exciting. Her science project had to be so spectacular that everyone would forget Damon's science project even existed!

Polly chewed her eraser. Just what *was* Damon's project, anyway?

Suddenly she noticed the house was strangely quiet. There were no sounds coming from the basement. No explosions rattling the windows. No clouds of smoke drifting up through the vents.

Polly went over to a small closet in the

hallway. Inside was a laundry chute that led right to the basement. She stuck her head into the closet and listened.

Silence.

Polly went back to her room and sat down at her desk. She tried to think more about her science project. But she couldn't concentrate. Her mind kept wandering back to Damon.

Finally, Polly snapped her notebook shut. She had to know what her stepbrother was doing.

The house was quiet as Polly crept back down to the basement. When she got to Damon's lab, she tried the handle. It was unlocked. She inched the door open and peeked inside.

Damon was hunched over his desk, writing. The single lightbulb burning overhead made his shadow look huge and twisted.

"No," Polly heard Damon mutter to himself. "Needs more . . . something else . . ." He scribbled on the paper. Polly could hear his pencil scratching.

Suddenly Damon sat back in his chair. "Yes!" he exclaimed. "I've got it! They'll be sorry they ever made fun of Damon Kreep. Soon everyone will answer to me!" He threw back his head and laughed.

A gasp escaped Polly's throat. Quickly, she clamped a hand over her mouth, but it was too late. Damon whipped around in his seat.

"Who's there?" he said.

Polly ducked back into the shadows.

Damon got up and came closer to the door. "Esme, is that you?" he asked, peering out into the darkness. "I *told* you, stay out of my lab!"

He slammed the door. As soon as Polly

heard the lock click she turned and fled for the stairs. There was no doubt about it now. Damon was up to something truly evil!

Polly had to find out what he was doing for his science project. She needed to get into the lab when Damon wasn't there. The fate of the school — and maybe even the world — depended on it!